THE
MAGIC
HEDGEHOG
LILY REDFERN
WORKBOOK PRESS
RECOMMENDED
LITERARY BOOK COMPETITION 2023

WORKBOOK PRESS LLC
187 E Warm Springs Rd,
Suite B285, Las Vegas, NV 89119, USA

Website: https://workbookpress.com/
Hotline: 1-888-818-4856
Email: admin@workbookpress.com

Ordering Information:
Quantity sales. Special discounts are available on quantity purchases by corporations, associations, and others.
For details, contact the publisher at the address above.

Library of Congress Control Number:
ISBN-13:   978-1-955459-53-2 (Paperback Version)
              978-1-955459-54-9 (Digital Version)

REV. DATE: 26/05/2021

It was a nice dry night and Julie was looking out her bedroom window before going to her bed. The lights kept going on and off every few minutes so she lookevd closer to see if there was anything in the garden at all.

First of all she did not see anything then when the light came on again here was a hedgehog going along the grass towards the cat food dish. She watched and the hedgehog went to the dish that the food was in and started to eat what was left in there, she was surprised at it eating that. She thought tomorrow I must ask what they eat.

Julie knew that they had a lot of fleas on them and she hoped that the cats would not go near them at all. She had two cats and they went out at night but not till later on.

Julie loved animals and when she went to bed she took one last look out and thought to herself what am I going to call this hedgehog?

When Julie lay in her bed she wondered as well if it was a male or a female hedgehog.

The next morning when Julie got up she looked out of the window and there was nothing there, the hedgehog was away as they come out more at night to get fed but you still see the odd one during the day. The cat meat was all finished so it must have been hungry if it ate all of that up. With Julie loving animals she collected books about them so she looked up the hedgehog to see what they ate and she was surprised to see cat and dog food written down as two of the things they ate as well as insects, minced meat, crushed cat biscuits, slugs, snails and chopped boiled eggs too.

She heard her mum shouting on her to get downstairs for breakfast so Julie went down all washed and dressed ready for school and sat down in the kitchen to get her breakfast before going to school. "What have you been doing this morning that you have been so long in coming down Julie", she asked her. "I was looking at a book about hedgehogs as I seen one in the garden last night" she told her mum. "It was eating all the cat meat and I did not know that they liked that at all", Julie said.

"Oh yes, they love all that sort of food" Julie's mum replied.

Julie sat and had her breakfast and then got up and put on her shoes and her coat and picked up her bag and said goodbye to her mum. The school was just along the road from her so she did not have far to go and she met with some of her friends on the way there.

When she was going along Hannah came and joined her she had a lot of animals at her house, so Julie was telling her about the hedgehog the night before and how she had looked up the book she had and it told her about the things that they ate. Hannah said to her "if you don't have enough cat food to put outside do you have any cat biscuits?", "yes" Julie replied. "Try them on some of them; you never know they might eat those too". "I wanted to find out if it is male or female, how will I do that?" Julie asked Hannah. "get a box and put the food into that and sit back and wait on the hedgehog coming and when it goes into the box to eat close it and take it down to the vet and they will tell you" Hannah said.

They got to school and went to their classes and did not see each other till lunch time. They sat down had a sandwich and a packet of crisps and a small bottle of juice and put the empty bottles and empty crisp packets into the bucket and went back to class again till it was time to come out.

They joined each other going back up the road again to go home and then Hannah said that she would come and join Julie and bring a box along with her to help her get the hedgehog.

When Julie got into the house she ran up the stairs and got changed into different clothes and laid her school clothes out for tomorrow at the side so she did not have to do it later on. She came down and said to her mum "Hannah is coming along and we are going outside to try and catch the hedgehog I seen last night" "ok, that is fine" she said to Julie "enjoy yourselves".

Hannah came along about 10 minutes later and she had a box with her. "Right do you have any cat food at all?" she said to Julie.

"Yes I have some opened up here for you and I have it in a bowl for it" she told Hannah. "Okay can we go into the garden now", Hannah said. "Yes I am all ready", replied Julie.

The garden was not too big, but it was ideal for wildlife as Julie's mum liked blackcurrant bushes and also climbing roses too so there were a lot of them round the garden as well as a hedge up one side where a lot of birds went into. There were gaps in the fence too so that way wildlife could come in and out of the garden and they could watch from the window.

The two girls went out into the back garden and sat outside for a few minutes. They both looked round to find the best place to put the box along with the food and Julie spotted a bush just across from them. "How if we put the box over there Hannah", and she pointed to the bush across from them "Oh that look's ideal", Hannah said. It was one that had been there for a long time now so it was really big.

Both Hannah and Julie went over with the box and also with the cat food in the bowl. Hannah placed the box down sideways so that it was open for the hedgehog to go into when it was going to get the food that Julie had there for it.

"Right Julie, can you put that bowl inside there as far to the back as possible", Hannah said. "No problem at all", Julie said. "Is this far enough back", she said to Hannah. "Yes, that's fine, now let's just sit back and wait to see if it comes back again", Hannah said.

So the two girls sat down waiting to see what would happen Julie had brought out some juice for them to drink while they were waiting. They sat for ages and all of a sudden here was the hedgehog coming along under the bushes.

It must have smelt the food they had put out for it. The two girls sat there watching as it went to the box and when it went inside it to go to the cat food at the back of it Julie got up along with Hannah and quietly went over and then grabbed the box and tipped it up so that they had the hedgehog trapped inside of the box.

"Right, let's get down to the vet so we can find out what it is for you" Hannah said to Julie. The two girls went down the road the vets was only about 5 doors away from Julie's house. When they went in they said to the receptionist "Is there any vet's in just now at all?" "Oh I think there is one and he is not doing anything just now girls", "would you like to go in and see him?" "Yes please" Julie said. "Can I ask you two what you have in the box?" the receptionist said. "It's a hedgehog, and we want to know if it is a male or female so that is why we came down" Julie said.

The receptionist went through the room and was away for a few minutes and the vet came through to them.

It was Ian that Julie knew and he was good with little animals.

"What have we got here girls?" Ian said, "it's a hedgehog that has been coming into the garden" Julie replied "I want to know if it is a male or female, and I thought if I brought it to you, you would be able to tell me" Julie replied.

Ian took the box from them and put it up onto the table but put a towel on the table first and then put some gloves on his hands so that he would not get pricked by the hedgehog as they were very prickly. They had at least 5000 spines, and then after a year each one drops out and a new one grows in. Then he took it out of the box and held it, he turned it over and told the girls "well you have a little male hedgehog here, and look it is changing colour too now, so you have a magic one, there is not very many of those about you are very lucky". "Is that all you want to know about it?" Ian the vet said to them. "Is it healthy?" Hannah asked. "Yes" he replied "very healthy".

"Just remember and wear gloves when you pick it up, otherwise you will get jagged and it will only change colour if you have been good that day and you will be able to make a wish when it changes colour". "Do we need to get special gloves at all?" Hannah asked the vet. "Get a pair of gardening gloves, they should do". Ian said to the girls. "But if you make a wish for the hedgehog it might just bring more into your garden, which would be better". Ian the vet said to Julie. "After all you do not see many hedgehogs now".

"But does it matter what colour it turns?" Julie asked Ian. "No" he replied.

The vet placed the hedgehog back in the box again for the girls to take away and the girls thanked him for doing that for them and went out the door. They went back up the road again back to the back garden and put the hedgehog back down under the bush and laid the dish of cat food down for it. "Well now we know what it is we need a name for it" Hannah said to Julie. "How about we call it Harry", and then we have Harry the hedgehog" Julie replied.

"That's a great idea" Hannah replied to Julie.

So Harry the hedgehog went over to the bush where the girls had placed the cat food and started to eat it. He cleared the plate and did not leave anything at all there.

The girls went back into the house to leave Harry and went upstairs watching him from the window to see what he was going to do next.

He went along by the grass and was eating things off there which must be insects and he would be getting moisture from the grass too. "Oh I must put out a bowl of water for Harry" Julie said to Hannah so that he always has something to drink when he comes into the garden.

Hannah looked at her watch and said to Julie "Well I must get back home for my tea, I will see you tomorrow so have fun tonight with Harry" "Oh I will, don't worry" Julie replied.

So Hannah went away to get her tea and then Julie went down the stairs for her tea as well. After that she went back up the stairs to watch Harry again to see if he was in the garden, but alas he was away he must have went somewhere else for a while.

Julie went and done her homework and went back outside again filling up the bowl with some more cat meat she put some cat biscuits at the side too just to see if Harry would eat them. After that she went away and got washed and ready for bed. Then she stood at the bedroom window when she seen the lights coming off and on all the time, Harry was in the back garden again, he was eating from the bowl again and drinking the water too.

Julie ended up making a home in her garden for Harry by going down the road the next day with Hannah with a bag and gathering a pile of old leaves and bits of wood so she brought all that back to the garden and put it in the corner where the other big bush was so that Harry would get shelter. Julie put all the leaves in a pile under the bush with the branches that she had gathered along with Hannah who helped her as well and got some logs too and sat them down. Some slugs and snails would go there and he would have something to eat and she put the bowl of fresh water up there too for him.

Each time Julie or Hannah picked up Harry when he changed colour they made a wish for another hedgehog to come in to the garden, and sure enough Ian the vet was right. Harry brought more hedgehogs to the garden.

Julie said to Hannah "Do you know they live for at least 5 years?" "No", Hannah replied and Harry stayed in the garden for a long time along with the other ones he had brought along.

The two girls loved going outside and making more nests in the garden for the other ones harry had brought along it kept them busy in the summer time.

THE END

www.ingramcontent.com/pod-product-compliance
Lightning Source LLC
Chambersburg PA
CBHW060806210726
48292CB00013B/1903